THIS BOOK BELONGS TO:

Samuel Biernar

Based on the TV series *Teenage Mutant Ninja Turtles*™ as seen on Fox and Cartoon Network®

SIMON SPOTLIGHT
An imprint of Simon & Schuster Children's Publishing Division
1230 Avenue of the Americas, New York, New York 10020
Meet Casey Jones; Look Out! It's Turtle Titan!; Friends Till the End!;
and *Lean, Green Smackdown Machine!* © 2004 Mirage Studios, Inc.
Blackout!; Four's a Crowd; and *Meet Leatherhead* © 2005 Mirage Studios, Inc.
Teenage Mutant Ninja Turtles™ is a trademark of Mirage Studios, Inc. All rights reserved.
SIMON SPOTLIGHT and colophon are registered trademarks of Simon & Schuster, Inc.
All rights reserved, including the right of reproduction in whole or in part in any form.
Manufactured in the United States of America
First Edition
2 4 6 8 10 9 7 5 3 1
ISBN 1-4169-0256-2

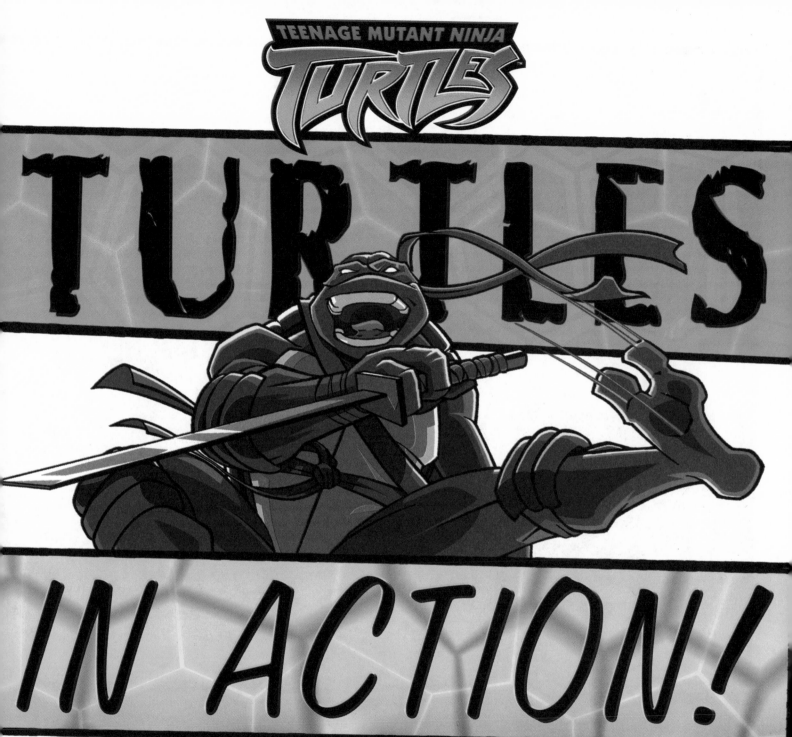

TEENAGE MUTANT NINJA TURTLES

TURTLES IN ACTION!

Simon Spotlight

New York   London   Toronto   Sydney

TABLE OF CONTENTS

In their secret underground lair the Teenage Mutant Ninja Turtles practiced their ninja skills.

Raphael and Michelangelo squared off for a friendly battle. Suddenly Raphael charged!

"Ha!" cried Michelangelo, flipping Raphael over his shoulder.

"Nice fall, bro," said Michelangelo.

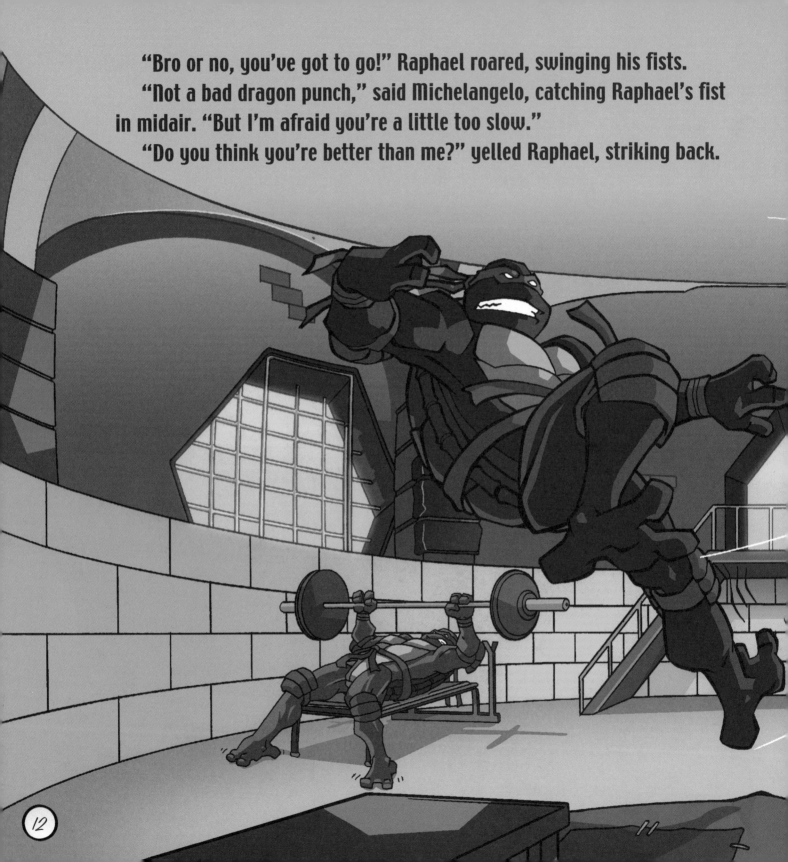

"Bro or no, you've got to go!" Raphael roared, swinging his fists.

"Not a bad dragon punch," said Michelangelo, catching Raphael's fist in midair. "But I'm afraid you're a little too slow."

"Do you think you're better than me?" yelled Raphael, striking back.

"I'm not better," Michelangelo said, dodging the blow. "You're just too cocky."
Now spinning out of control, Raphael crashed into a wooden table, smashing it to pieces. The raging Turtle grabbed a leg from the broken table and swung it like a club.

Raphael was ready to swing again. But this time Splinter grabbed his wrist.

"You must remember that anger is a monster that will hurt you from within," advised Splinter. "You must use self-control. Find balance in all things."

Raphael heard his master's words and knew they were true. Suddenly ashamed, he dropped the club and stumbled outside.

High above the city on the roof of an abandoned warehouse Raphael gazed out at the starry night sky. He felt so ashamed for losing his temper that he just wanted to curl up in his shell and never come out again.

Meanwhile in a rundown apartment not too far away there lived the one man who was even more hotheaded than Raphael. His name was Casey Jones.

"The Purple Dragons are still on the rampage," said the television announcer.

Casey Jones had heard enough. He stormed over to his closet and dug out his sports equipment. He slid a hockey mask over his face, put on his gloves, and grabbed a hockey stick.

"Those Purple Dragons will pay for their crimes!" he roared.

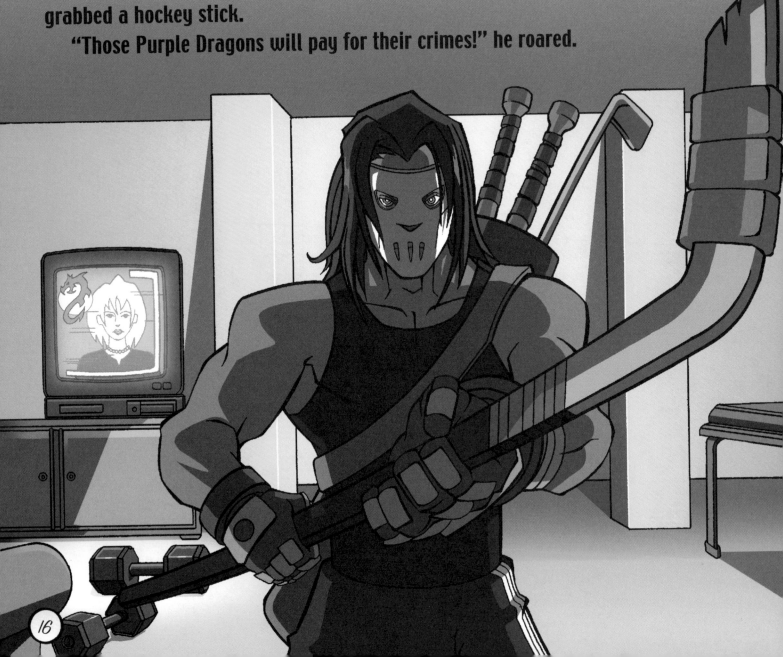

"Hand over the purse and we promise not to hurt you," snarled a Purple Dragon member. The muggers were about to snatch the purse from the lady when they heard a strange sound.

"Oh, Purple Draaaaa-gons! Come out to plaaaaay!"

Casey Jones stepped out of the shadows.

"Bring it on!" said Casey as he spun his hockey stick.

The punks charged. One by one Casey took the punks down until the leader was the only one left standing.

"I surrender! Don't hurt me," begged the Purple Dragon. But Casey Jones stood over him and raised his stick.

"I'm putting you punks out of business once and for all!" he cried.

From the rooftop Raphael spotted the action. When he saw Casey Jones attack the muggers Raphael grinned.

"This is gonna be good!" he said.

But then Raphael saw that the hockey-masked man was ready to clobber one of the muggers—*after* the man had given up.

"That guy's out of control!" cried Raphael. "I have to stop him."

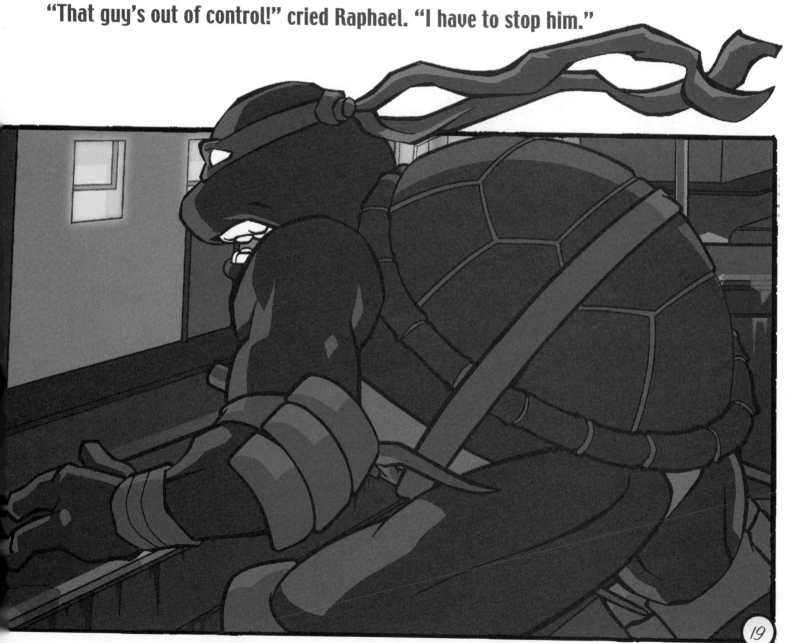

Raphael leaped from the rooftop and landed on a dumpster. Then he rushed to Casey Jones and grabbed his wrist to stop the blow.

"Easy there, cowboy!" the Turtle said. "They're down. It's over."

In the confusion the Purple Dragons saw their chance to escape and ran away.

"Let go! They're getting away!" cried the masked man as he broke free.

"Wait!" cried Raphael, chasing Casey Jones, who was chasing the Purple Dragons. Casey caught up with a Purple Dragon and knocked him down. He was ready to clobber the man, but Raphael arrived in time to stop him again.

"I *told* you to cool it pal," said the Ninja Turtle.

"Yeah?" Casey Jones shot back. "Well, I told you to stay out of my way. But since your ears don't work, I'll have to get my point across *another* way!"

"You're doing the right thing," the Turtle said. "But you're going about it all wrong. What if you grab the wrong guy? You could get in trouble."

"You're the one who's in trouble!" yelled Casey. He pulled back his stick and swung, sending the Turtle crashing into a bunch of garbage cans.

"Goal!" cried Casey.

Dazed, Raphael crawled out of the garbage in time to see Casey Jones hop onto the back of a motorcycle.

"And there's more where that came from!" yelled Casey. "If you want a rematch, I'll be in Central Park waiting for you. Bye-bye!"

Raphael stumbled back to the Turtles' secret lair.

"Wow!" said Michelangelo. "What happened to you?"

"It's a long story," said Raphael. "But first I wanted to say I'm sorry for blowing my top."

Michelangelo punched Raphael's shoulder. "Don't sweat it, bro."

Then Raphael told them all about Casey Jones. "We have to go to Central Park right now and stop him before he hurts someone."

"Maybe we should ask Master Splinter first," said Leonardo.

"And have him stop us!" Raphael cried. "No way."

"Ahem," said Splinter, twitching his nose.

"Busted!" sighed Michelangelo.

"It is dangerous for you to walk among the humans," Splinter said, handing Michelangelo a set of keys. "Take the truck!"

Minutes later a strange noise was heard from the inside of an abandoned warehouse. Then a rusty garage door rumbled open. Bright headlights lit up the dark streets.

Finally tires squealed and rubber burned as the new turbo-powered Teenage Mutant Ninja Turtles Battle Wagon burst out of the garage!

"It's Casey Jones!" yelled Raphael, pointing. "Floor it, Don. Keep up with him!"

"You can catch up to him yourself, Raph!" Donatello replied. "I whipped up a little something special for you. Hop in the back and check it out."

Raphael raced to the rear of the Battle Wagon. He gasped in surprise.

"You are *the Turtle,* Don!" he cried.

A moment later the superpowered ShellCycle burst out of the back of the Battle Wagon.

Soon Raphael caught up with Casey Jones. Raphael cut the spokes out of Casey's rear wheel. The cycle flipped over and crashed. Casey made a soft landing in some bushes.

"I can't believe I just got my butt kicked by a frog," he moaned.

"Turtle," said Raphael, correcting him. "Look, I'll be glad to help you stop the Purple Dragons. But you have to use a little self-control."

"No way," said Casey Jones. "When I was a kid they burned down my father's store. So don't tell me how to deal with the Purple Dragons!"

Raphael suddenly remembered Splinter's words.

"But your anger makes you act just like them!" he told Casey Jones. "You must find balance in all things."

"Isn't this nice!" said a sinister voice.

Raphael and Casey Jones found themselves surrounded by the Purple Dragons.

Lucky for them, the rest of the Turtles arrived just in time.

"Friends of yours?" asked Casey.

"My brothers," said Raphael.

"I can see the family resemblance!" Casey said with a chuckle.

Just then the Purple Dragons attacked.

"Incoming goons!" warned Donatello.

The fight was on, and it was fast and furious . . . but the Purple Dragons never even had a chance!

In a whirl of fists and kicks the Teenage Mutant Ninja Turtles—with the help of Casey Jones—took the Purple Dragons down.

When it was all over, Raphael turned to Casey Jones. "I'm glad I met you, crazy man."
Casey nodded. "I think I learned something."
Raphael smiled. "You mean balance? Self-control?"
Casey playfully punched Raphael's arm. Raphael punched him back, just a little harder. Soon Casey Jones and Raphael were wrestling on the ground. The other Turtles looked at the brawlers and shook their heads.
"Let me know when you guys are finished," said Michelangelo. "I'm starving."

TEENAGE MUTANT NINJA

TURTLES™

LOOK OUT! IT'S TURTLE TITAN!

"We're supposed to be practicing the ninja art of invisibility, Mikey," whispered a voice from the shadows.

"I know, Leonardo," replied Michelangelo, not bothering to whisper. "But I'm tired of sneaking around all the time. I wish we could fight crime out in the open."

Across the street from the Turtles a building had caught fire.

"Hey, look!" exclaimed Donatello.

"We have to help that kid!" cried Michelangelo.

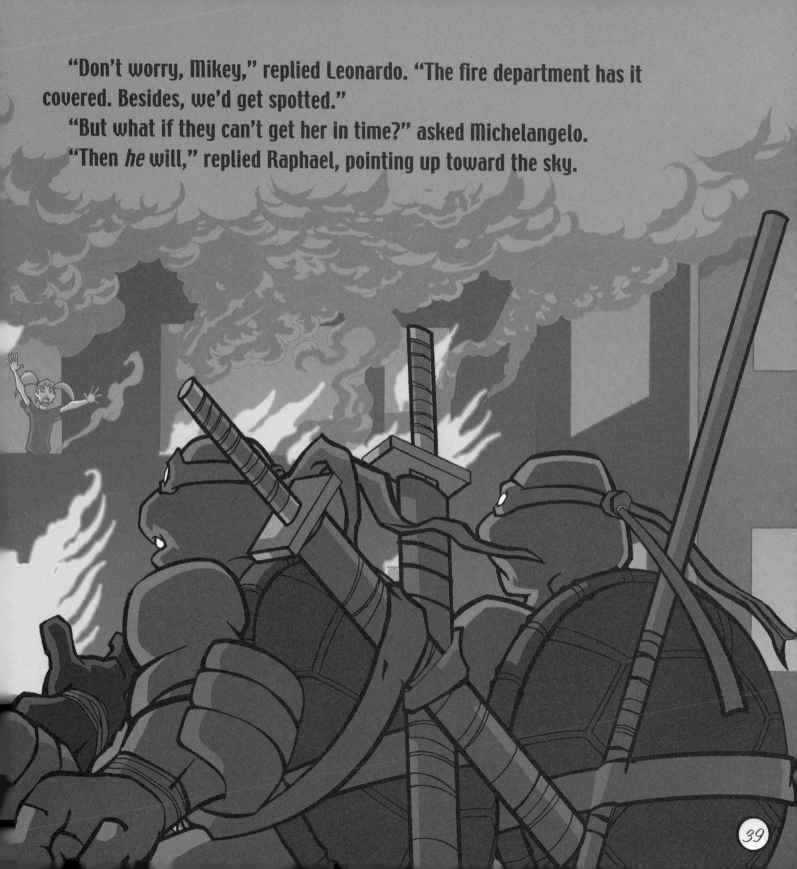

"Don't worry, Mikey," replied Leonardo. "The fire department has it covered. Besides, we'd get spotted."

"But what if they can't get her in time?" asked Michelangelo.

"Then *he* will," replied Raphael, pointing up toward the sky.

"Wow . . . it's really him. The Silver Sentry!" Michelangelo shouted.

The Turtles watched as the Silver Sentry flew straight into the building fire, swooped up the child, and set her down on the sidewalk.

"See, now there's a guy who doesn't have to stick to the shadows," said Michelangelo. "Look how much he's able to do."

"That's it, dudes! We should become superheroes!" exclaimed Michelangelo, impressed by the Silver Sentry's actions.

Donatello couldn't believe what his brother was saying. "I think you've got your bandanna on too tight, Mikey. The oxygen's not making it to your brain."

Back home at their sewer lair Michelangelo brought up his superhero idea again. "Superheroes never have to hold back because they're afraid someone might see them. And wouldn't it be nice to get a little credit for the good we do?" he asked.

Master Splinter spoke. "Your intentions are noble, Michelangelo. But you must never forget who you are. You are a ninja. Ninjas operate in the shadows."

"But couldn't we accomplish so much more out in the open?" asked Michelangelo. "There are many paths, my son," replied Splinter. "You must choose the one that is true to yourself."

Later that night Michelangelo went out on his own to fight crime. He had made a superhero costume out of old clothes and junk borrowed from his friend April O'Neil's antique store.

"Intro-ducing . . . Turtle Titan!" announced Michelangelo as he struck a heroic pose.

Michelangelo noticed that there was a robbery taking place at Crazy Manny's Electronic Store.

"Cowabunga!" cried Turtle Titan, as he swung toward the scene of the robbery in progress.

"Crazy Manny, why are you robbing your own store?" asked Turtle Titan. The man stared blankly and said nothing.

"Hey, what's that on your neck?" the superhero asked Crazy Manny, brushing a strange-looking insect from the storeowner's neck.

"Why are you robbing my store?!" exclaimed Crazy Manny, confused and frightened.

"Wait, *I'm* not breaking into your store. *You* were!" replied Turtle Titan. The hero then turned his gaze toward the strange insect scuttling away.

"Get out!" shouted Crazy Manny. "Police!"

And with that, Turtle Titan ran out of the store before the police showed up.

Later that night Turtle Titan tried to stop an out-of-control bus.

"Gee, this is crazy," the superhero said to himself, as he climbed inside the moving bus. "What's up with people tonight, anyway?"

"Hey, driver, step on the brake!" yelled Turtle Titan. But the driver stared blankly, said nothing, and did nothing—except to continue stepping on the gas pedal.

"Aw, no!" cried Turtle Titan. "This bus is going to cannonball right into the East River, and there's nothing I can do about it!"

Suddenly, Silver Sentry appeared and carried the bus to safety.

"Silver Sentry! You saved our butts!" exclaimed Turtle Titan gratefully.

"No problem, citizen," replied the superhero.

Turtle Titan had removed the strange robotic insect from the bus driver's neck and handed it to Silver Sentry. "Someone's been controlling people with these things."

Silver Sentry examined the robo-bug. "This looks like the work of my arch-nemesis, Doctor Malignus. I think it's time I paid him a visit."

"Count me in!" cried Turtle Titan.

"I appreciate your help, kid, but you're in way over your head," said Silver Sentry. "Keep yourself out of sight while I deal with Malignus."

Turtle Titan watched as the Silver Sentry flew off to a warehouse used by his archenemy.

"You don't understand!" shouted Turtle Titan. "I became a superhero so that I *wouldn't* have to hide in the shadows anymore!"

"Ah, what does *he* know?" And with that said, the Turtle Titan ran across the Brooklyn Bridge and soon arrived at the villain's warehouse nearly out of breath.

"Gee, you'd think the arch-villain of a major superhero could afford a better place," Turtle Titan whispered to himself, as he studied his surroundings.

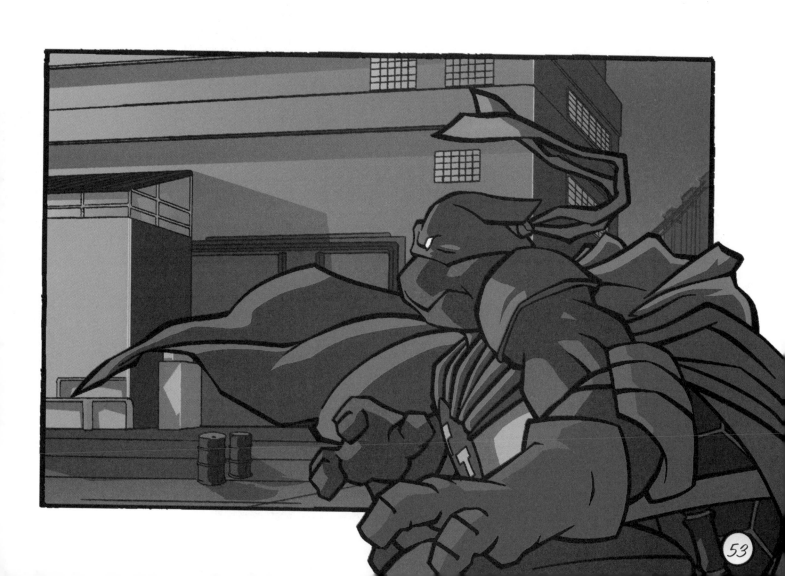

"Doctor Malignus, I presume?" asked Turtle Titan bravely. "Uh-oh . . . what have you done to Silver Sentry?"

"Nothing much. I've simply put him completely under my control. He's now my superpuppet," said the villain. "He'll do anything I say. And I say . . . destroy that turtle!"

"Ooof!" exhaled Turtle Titan, the breath momentarily knocked out of him. "There's only one thing to do—I've got to be ninja-fast and try to nab that nasty robo-bug!"

"Nice move, Turtle Titan," said a thankful Silver Sentry, now free from the arch-villain's mind control.

"It's over, Malignus. You've lost," said the superhero, as he turned to face his enemy.

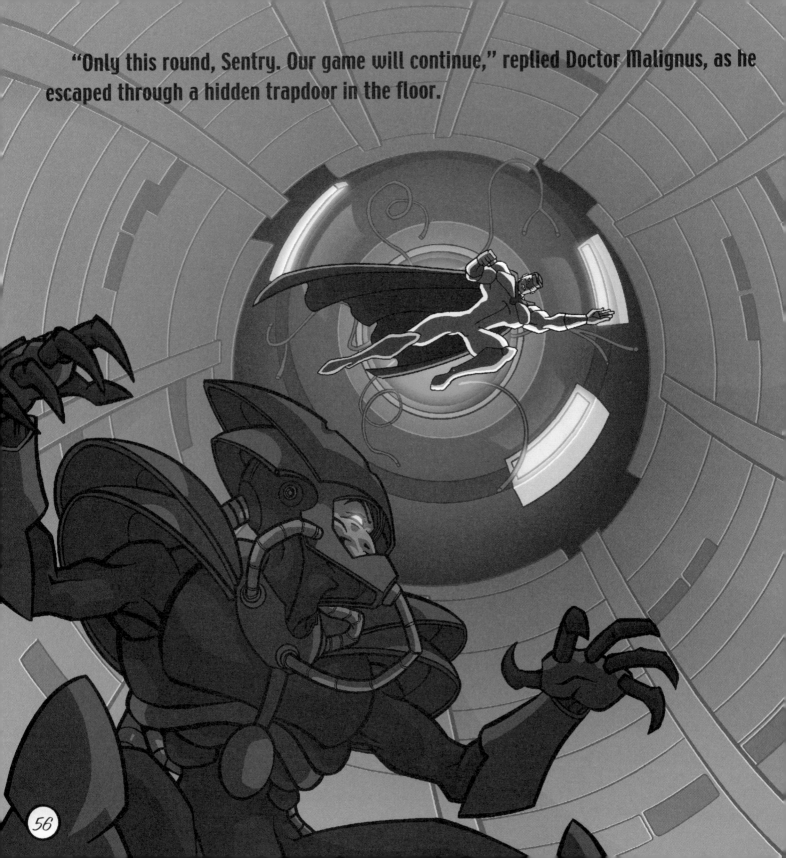

"Only this round, Sentry. Our game will continue," replied Doctor Malignus, as he escaped through a hidden trapdoor in the floor.

56

Who needs a shield and grapple? thought Michelangelo, as he emerged from the shadows no longer wearing his Turtle Titan costume.

"Game over, Malignus!" said Michelangelo. It was the last thing the villain heard before the Ninja Turtle's flying dropkick stopped him cold.

Afterward Michelangelo thought about his night's adventure.
"I guess I can do a lot more good for this town working from the shadows—the only way a Ninja Turtle can," he said to himself. "*That* is my true path."

"I remember the first time I saw you, Angel," said Raphael as he reached for another slice of pizza. "It was right after you helped the Purple Dragons rob that appliance store. You were waiting outside. I thought you looked pretty cool. Way too cool to be hanging out with a no-good group like the Purple Dragons."

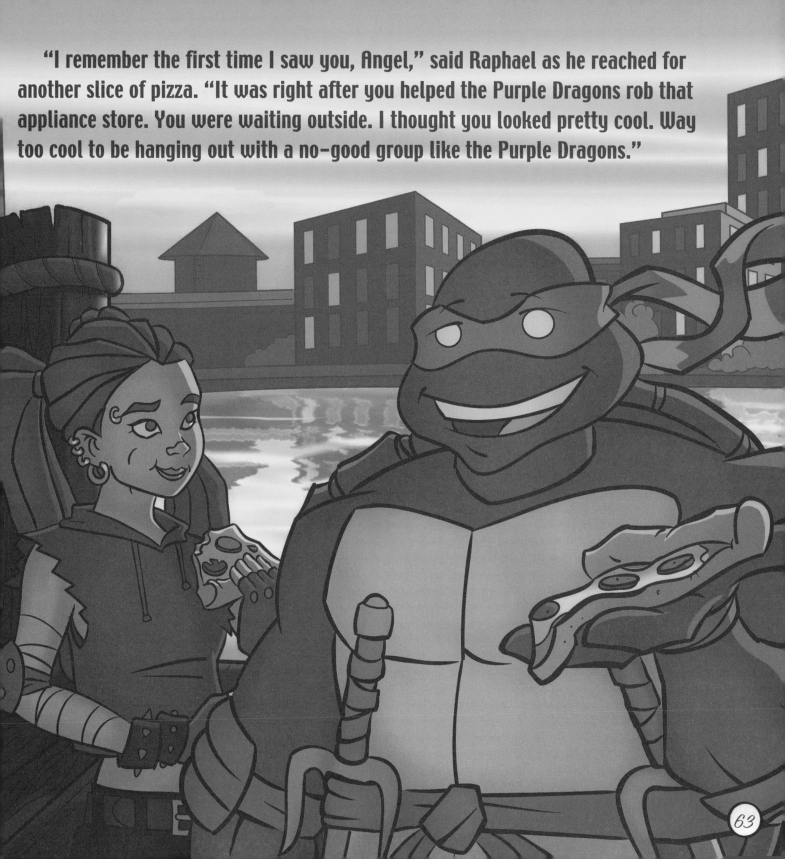

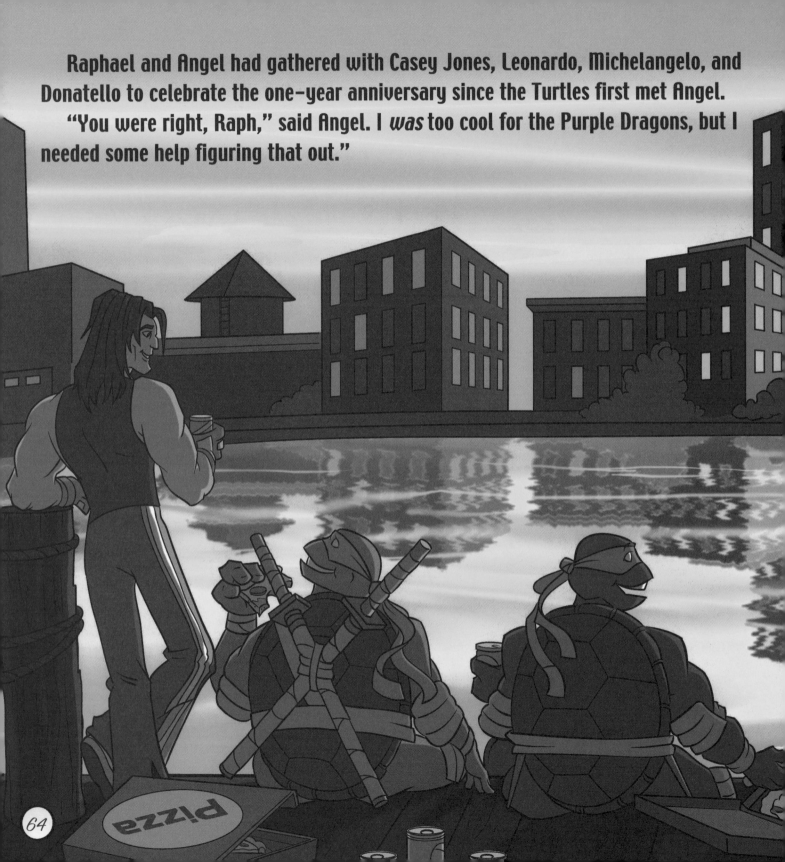

Raphael and Angel had gathered with Casey Jones, Leonardo, Michelangelo, and Donatello to celebrate the one-year anniversary since the Turtles first met Angel. "You were right, Raph," said Angel. I *was* too cool for the Purple Dragons, but I needed some help figuring that out."

"Hey, what are friends for!" said Leonardo.

Angel grinned. "I have to admit, though, that when I first got a good look at you and your brothers I thought you were all, well, pretty *funky* looking!"

"Yeah, well, that was a pretty funky night," said Casey. "It started off simple enough, with me and the boys catching the Dragons red-handed in the middle of ripping off that store."

"I remember Raphael asked the Dragons, 'Now, class, who can tell me what you've done wrong?'" continued Casey.

"And then I said, 'You mean besides being badly dressed, lawbreaking, good-for-nothing low-life street punks?'"

The group laughed.

"Like I said," continued Casey, "it was a simple enough matter that night. At least until I spotted Angel.

"She bugged out when she recognized me. She asked me why I was interfering. I remember looking her straight in the eye and saying: 'I'm trying to stop you from making the biggest mistake of your life.'

"Then Angel said something about the Dragons being like family and ran off."

"But I promised her Grandma that I'd look out for her. So I wasn't going to let her get away that easily. The next night I decided to keep an eye out on her apartment just in case some Purple Dragon punks showed up."

"Imagine my surprise when I saw Angel sneak out in the middle of the night! I was so mad that I wanted to jump out and yell at her, but I remembered Splinter telling me to always look before I leap. So instead I decided to follow her. And Angel led me right to the Purple Dragons's headquarters!"

"I followed Angel over to the fight ring," Casey said. "I knew she didn't stand a chance. I had to do something. So I did the one thing I know best."

"Casey was way outnumbered," said Angel, continuing the story, "plus that one guy was humongous—the one named Hun."

"'Tie Jones up,' Hun rumbled, with a voice like an avalanche. 'We'll play some more with him later,'" said Angel.

"Casey looked up at me and whispered, 'Go get my *real* friends.' Then he passed out. Of course he meant you guys—the funky bunch."

"It didn't take me long to find you guys. Actually you found me first, approaching me silently from the darkness like living shadows. I explained what had happened to Casey and how we had to save him from the Dragons. I remember *you* answering, Michelangelo. 'Of course, that's what friends are for,' you said. Simple as that."

"One of the first lessons Splinter taught us is that friends and family are supposed to be there for each other—at all times," said Leonardo. "It *is* that simple."
The Turtles looked at each other in agreement. Then Donatello started laughing.

"What's so funny?" asked Leonardo.

"I was just remembering what happened when Angel tried to get us to wear disguises before heading out after Casey," Donatello said.

"Remember?" asked Donatello. "We went through all that used clothing from April's antique store. It was like dressing up for Halloween!

"Then Angel intervened. She dressed us up and showed us how to act so we would fit in, and then hustled us over to the Purple Dragons's club."

"At the club," continued Donatello, "Leo and Raph entered the steel fight cage to keep Hun busy. Meanwhile Angel led Mike and me up to the club's overhead catwalks in order to free Casey, who was hanging upside down from the ceiling."

"From the catwalk Angel turned the spotlight directly into the eyes of Casey's guards. Then Mike and I could finish the job with perfectly timed flying drop-kicks."

79

"Casey barely had time to thank Angel when we heard what sounded like a ton of steel bars striking the cement floor. We looked down and saw that Hun had pulled down the steel cage that Leo and Raph had been in.

"Fortunately for us Hun wasn't very smart," said Donatello. "He had also pulled the cage down on top of himself!"

"I ran down from the catwalk just in time to see Casey standing over Hun about to hurt him. 'This one's for my father,' snarled Casey. But before Casey could do anything, Angel reached out to stop him.

"'Angel! What are you doing?' Casey yelled, as Angel pulled him away from Hun.

"'Stopping you from doing something you might regret,' replied Angel.

"Casey stared at her. 'You're right,' he said. 'Thanks.'

"'No problem,' she replied. 'That's what friends are for.'"

"Right," echoed Casey, "that *is* what friends are for!"

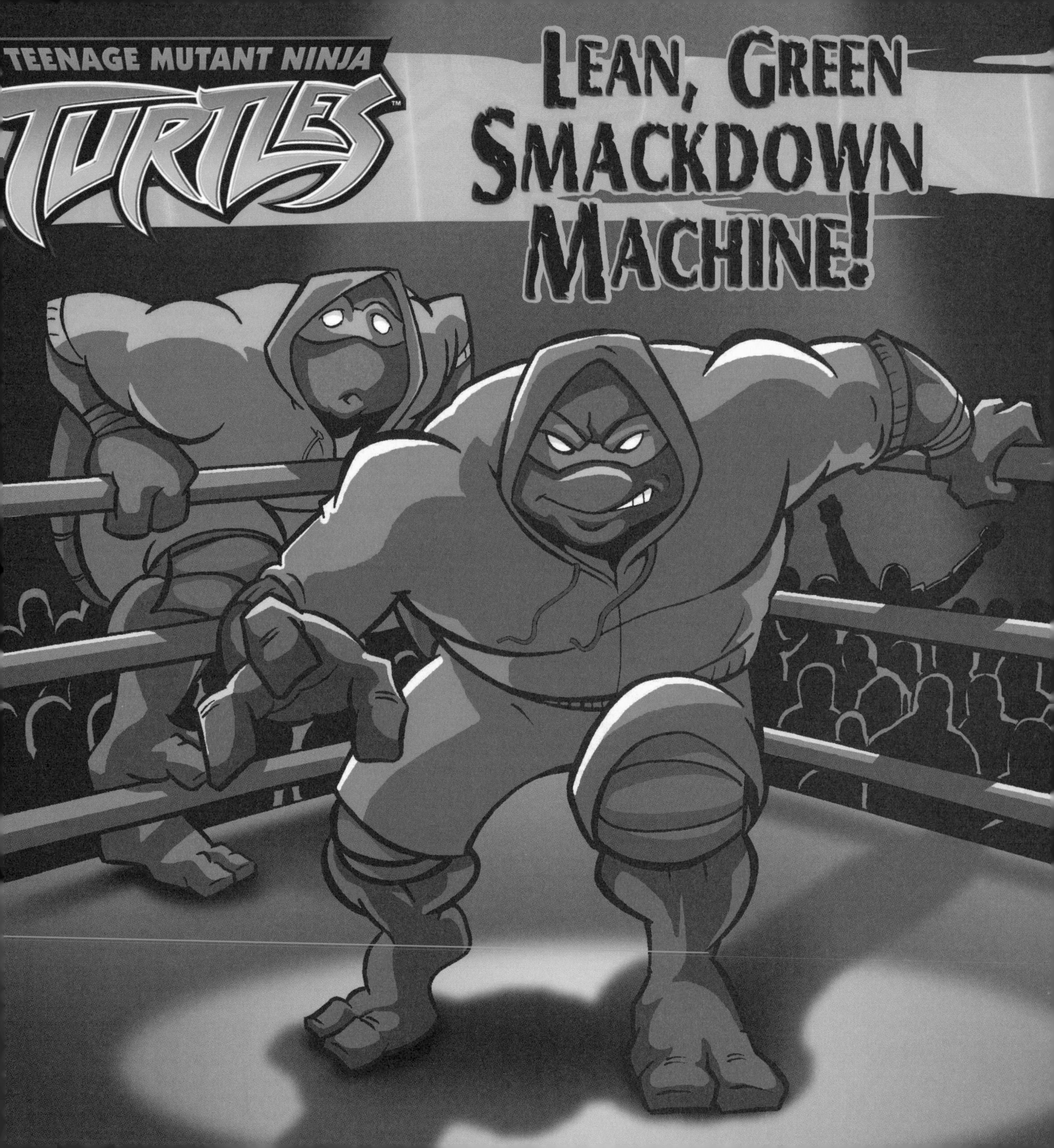
TEENAGE MUTANT NINJA
TURTLES™
LEAN, GREEN
SMACKDOWN
MACHINE!

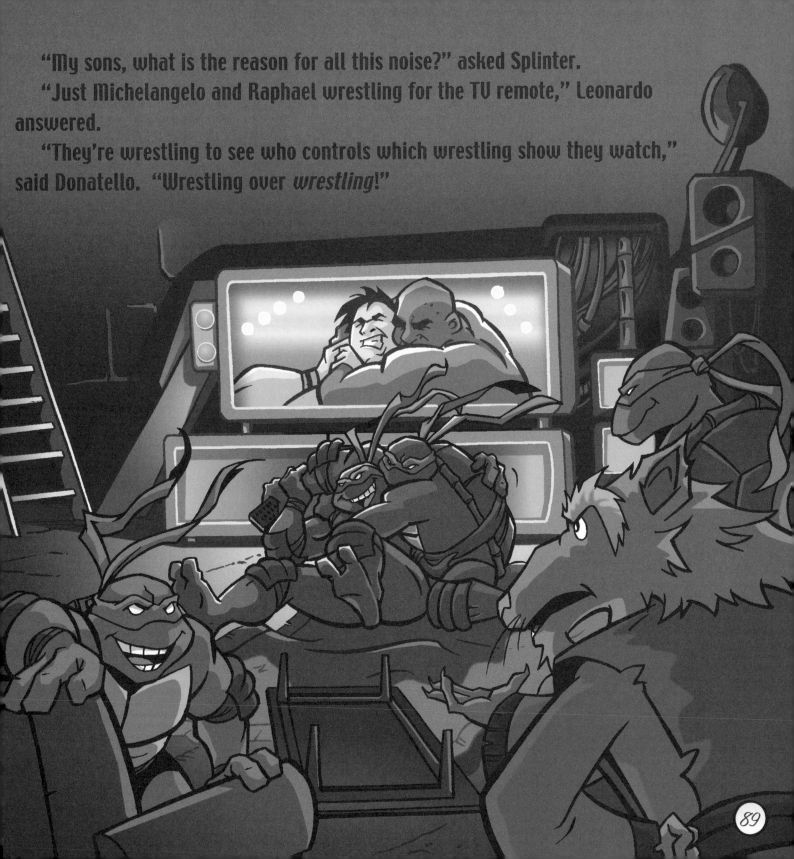

"My sons, what is the reason for all this noise?" asked Splinter.

"Just Michelangelo and Raphael wrestling for the TV remote," Leonardo answered.

"They're wrestling to see who controls which wrestling show they watch," said Donatello. "Wrestling over *wrestling*!"

Just then a TV commercial caught everyone's attention.

"You heard me right, wrestling fan," said the man. "An amateur wrestling match. Tonight at the Ronald Rump Civic Center. Open to everyone and anyone."

Then with a smirk the man added, "Anyone with enough *guts.* Do *you* have enough guts, wrestling fan?"

"We've got the guts!" Raphael shouted.

"And the *skillingest* skills!" added Michelangelo. "Piece of cake, bro!"

"Yeah, we're there!" agreed Raphael. "Now all we have to do is come up with some costumes."

"Get ready to rumble!" they both yelled.

Michelangelo and Raphael quickly came up with their wrestling outfits and headed to the Ronald Rump Civic Center.

"I like your look, boys," said Lon Jing, the wrestling promoter. "Sorta mutant, sorta turtle, definitely green. Green and lean. I've got it: the Lean, Green Machine!"

"How about . . . the Lean, Green Smackdown Machine?" asked Michelangelo.

"Even better," answered Mr. Jing. "Now follow me."

Mr. Jing led the two brothers into the wrestling arena.
"I'm pumped!" said Raphael when he saw the huge crowd.
"Me too!" Michelangelo said. "This is way cooler than seeing it on TV!"

In the ring the referee introduced the wrestlers. "In this corner, weighing more than most automobiles, are two brothers—Hun and Ahnold—the human avalanches otherwise known as . . . the Massive Man-Mountains!"

"And in this corner," he said, pointing to the two Turtles, "looking fit and mean . . . the Lean, Green Smackdown Machine!"

"Uh-oh," Michelangelo whispered to Raphael, "the guy with the beard is Shredder's right-hand man, Hun!"

The bell rang, and suddenly Hun and Ahnold had the Turtles up in the air! "Looks like a double twirly bird, folks," said the referee. "The Massive Man-Mountains are playing helicopter with the Smackdown Machine, both of whom are beginning to look a little too green, if you know what I mean."

Crack!

Raphael and Michelangelo struck each other—hard.

"That had to hurt, ladies and gentlemen," said the referee.

"Ha. Was that not fun, my brother?" said Hun, laughing.

"Ha. Big fun, my brother," Ahnold replied. "Come, let us have more fun with these little green men."

Michelangelo and Raphael kept getting pounded by Hun and Ahnold.

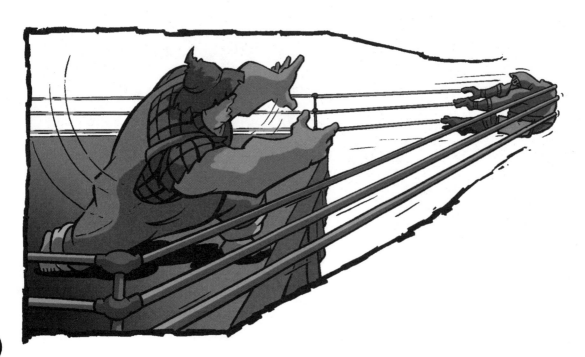

Raphael groaned. "We need a plan, Mikey. We're getting our butts kicked."

"Too bad ninjitsu isn't allowed in wrestling," moaned Michelangelo.

Suddenly Raphael had an idea. "You're right, Mikey!" he exclaimed. "We can't use ninjitsu, but we *can* use another form of our ninja training. Come on, get up."

"Look," Raphael whispered, "we can use one of Splinter's lessons: 'Turn your enemy's size and strength to your advantage.' Remember that one?"

"Right! We can turn their size and strength *against each other*!" Michelangelo whispered back.

With a loud scream—"HAI-YA!"—the two Turtles leaped toward their opponents.

"Hey, no fair, little man," said Ahnold as he tripped over Michelangelo.

"All's fair in love and war . . . and wrestling," said Raphael, making the same move on Hun.

"On the count of three," said the referee. "One."

"I cannot move," Ahnold said to Hun. "Get off me, my brother."

"Two," counted off the referee.

"I cannot move," said Hun. "These little men are holding us down."

"Three!" yelled the referee.

"And the winners are . . . the Lean, Green Smackdown Machine!" proclaimed the referee. The crowd cheered wildly.

"Check out this cool trophy belt," Raphael crowed.

"Cowabunga!" Michelangelo yelled to the crowd.

A short while later the two Turtles made their way home.

"We watched you guys on TV," said Donatello. "You had us worried for a while there."

"Excellent trophy," Leonardo said, "but it makes me wonder."

"Wonder what?" Raphael asked.

"It makes me wonder who will be wearing it," said Leonardo.

Raphael and Michelangelo looked at each other.
"I will," Raphael declared.
"No," said Michelangelo, "I will."
"Then get ready to rumble," Raphael told Michelangelo.

Just then Splinter entered the room. "Now what is the reason for the noise this time?" he asked.

"Just Michelangelo and Raphael wrestling again," Leonardo replied.

"*Now* they're wrestling to see who gets to wear their wrestling belt," said Donatello. "Always wrestling over wrestling."

"Ah, but at least this time *we* have the remote, my sons," Splinter said, turning on a Bruce Lee movie.

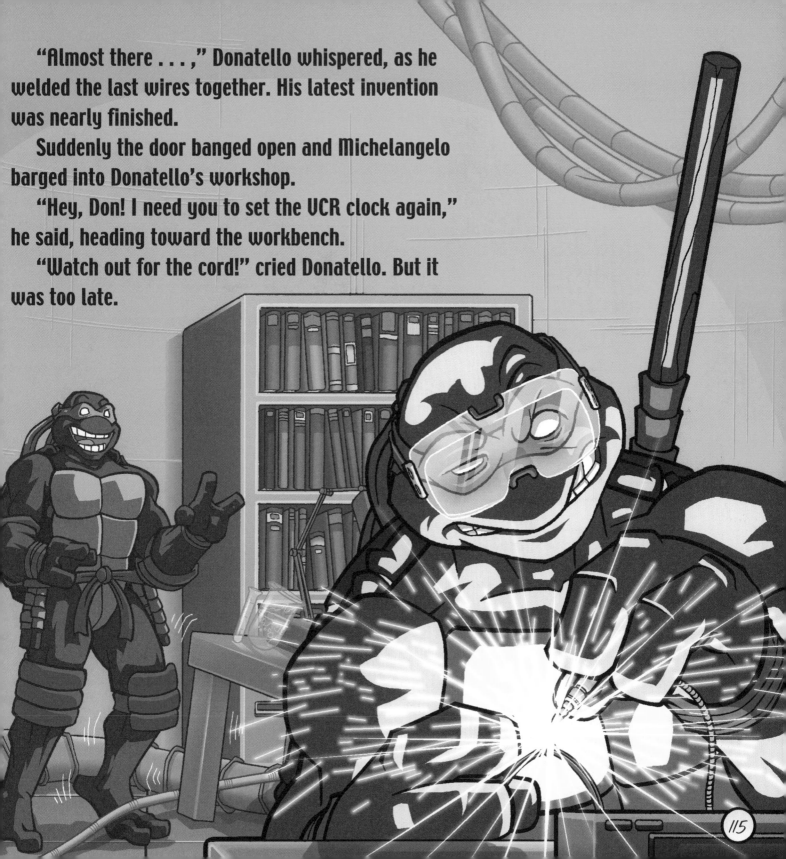

"Almost there . . . ," Donatello whispered, as he welded the last wires together. His latest invention was nearly finished.

Suddenly the door banged open and Michelangelo barged into Donatello's workshop.

"Hey, Don! I need you to set the VCR clock again," he said, heading toward the workbench.

"Watch out for the cord!" cried Donatello. But it was too late.

115

CRASH! BANG! BOOM!

Everything on Donatello's workbench came crashing down. The Turtles escaped the explosion just in time—but Donatello's invention hadn't been so lucky. Donatello stared at the mess in horror.

"Oops," said Michelangelo.

"Look what you've done, Mikey!" shouted Donatello. "My new invention is ruined!"

"I'm really sorry," Michelangelo said. "Is there anything I can do?"

"You can learn to knock first," snapped Donatello, storming out into the hallway.

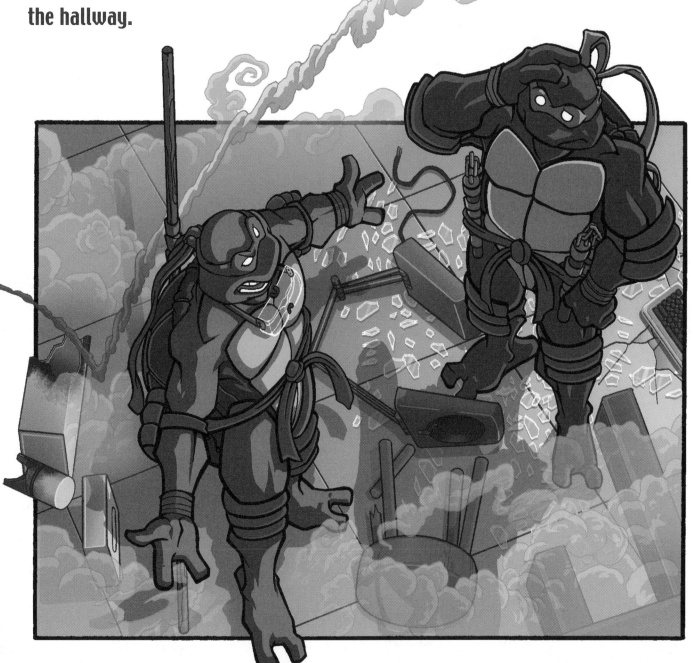

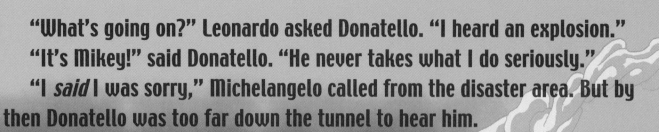

"What's going on?" Leonardo asked Donatello. "I heard an explosion."

"It's Mikey!" said Donatello. "He never takes what I do seriously."

"I *said* I was sorry," Michelangelo called from the disaster area. But by then Donatello was too far down the tunnel to hear him.

"Hey, Don, wait up," Leonardo called. "Don't you think you were a little hard on Mikey? He didn't mean to—"

"Shh," Donatello said, forgetting all about the explosion. "I hear voices."

The two Turtles listened closely.

"You're right, Don," Leonardo whispered. "There are people here in the sewers."

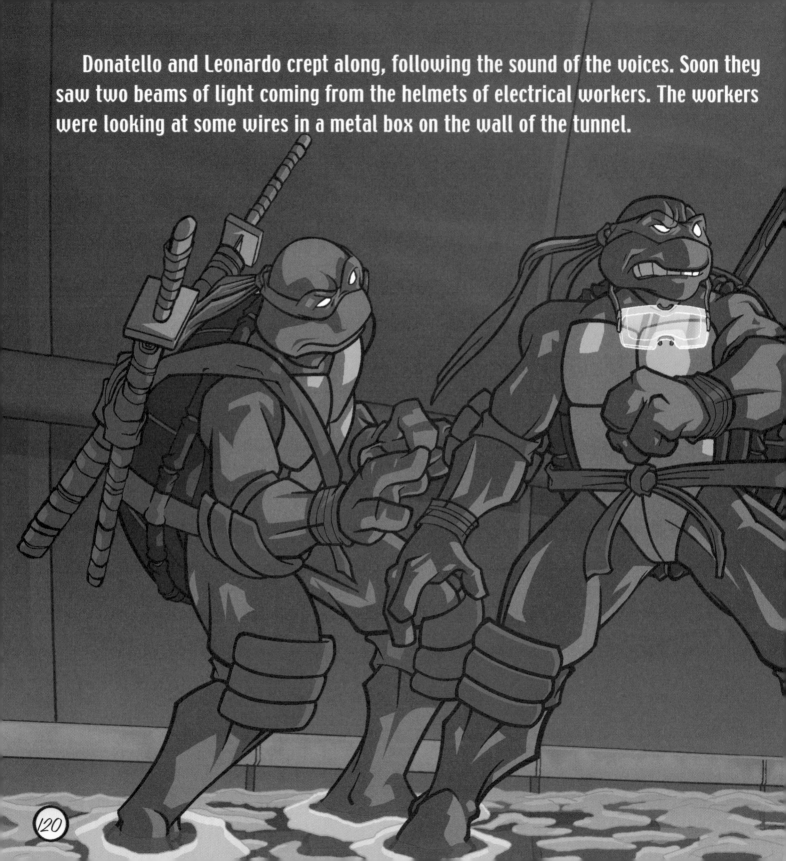

Donatello and Leonardo crept along, following the sound of the voices. Soon they saw two beams of light coming from the helmets of electrical workers. The workers were looking at some wires in a metal box on the wall of the tunnel.

"Those are the city's power lines!" Donatello whispered to Leonardo.

"Shh," said Leonardo. "Listen."

"Bob, we'll never finish repairing these power lines in time!" said one worker, sounding worried.

"We have to, Sam," said the other worker. "Otherwise half the city will lose its power."

"I hope they know what they're doing," Donatello whispered to Leonardo. "That power grid controls the city hospital. If it loses power, patients could die!"

121

"Sam, quick!" said Bob. "Hand me the drill."

Sam picked up a drill and flicked on the switch. Nothing happened.

"Let me try," said Bob. As he reached for the drill, it suddenly turned on and slipped away from them.

"Look out!" cried Donatello—but he wasn't fast enough. The drill sailed through the air and severed a drooping power line before landing in the water below.

"Sam's going to get fried!" cried Donatello, bursting forth from the shadows. He scooped up Sam and jumped up to grab hold of a ceiling pipe. Bob was nearby, clinging to a ladder on the tunnel wall.

"Leo! I need a little help!" Donatello hollered. "Sam is starting to slip!"

Leonardo, who had been gripping another pipe, walked his hands from pipe to pipe toward Donatello and Sam.

Bob couldn't believe his eyes. "Giant turtles in the sewer?" he muttered weakly. "What is the world coming to?"

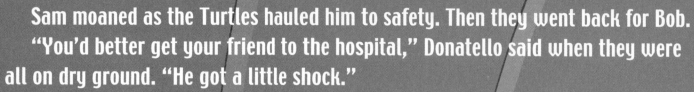

Sam moaned as the Turtles hauled him to safety. Then they went back for Bob.

"You'd better get your friend to the hospital," Donatello said when they were all on dry ground. "He got a little shock."

"But what about the power?" Bob asked nervously. "If it doesn't get fixed—"

"Trust us," Donatello said. "We'll take care of it."

"Right," Bob mumbled. "I always go around trusting giant turtles. Maybe *I'm* the one who needs the doctor!"

CAUTION
HIGH VOLTAGE

SHOC
HART

Leonardo helped Bob carry Sam up a ladder and through a manhole that led to the street. "Thanks for your help," said Bob, as he disappeared through the manhole. "Oh, no!"

"What is it?" asked Leonardo. He poked his head out of the manhole and gasped—the city was almost as dark as the tunnels below!

Meanwhile Donatello was busy studying the power grid.

"This is going to be a big job," he said.

"The bigger, the better!" said a voice. It was Michelangelo! "I heard men's voices and came to see what was going on," he said. "But if you think I might mess things up . . ."

"We can use your help," said Donatello. "Just watch your step!"

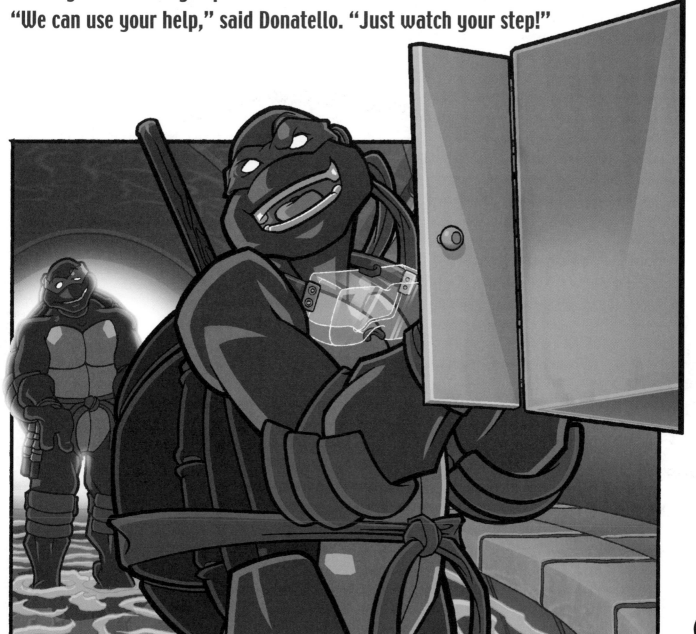

"The city lights are fading fast!" Leonardo said when he returned.

"We have no time to lose," said Donatello, putting on his safety goggles. "Leo, Mikey—I need you to rescue the loose power line and bring it back to me. Remember to watch where you step!"

"All right!" Michelangelo shouted, as he and Leonardo got to work. "It's Turtle time!"

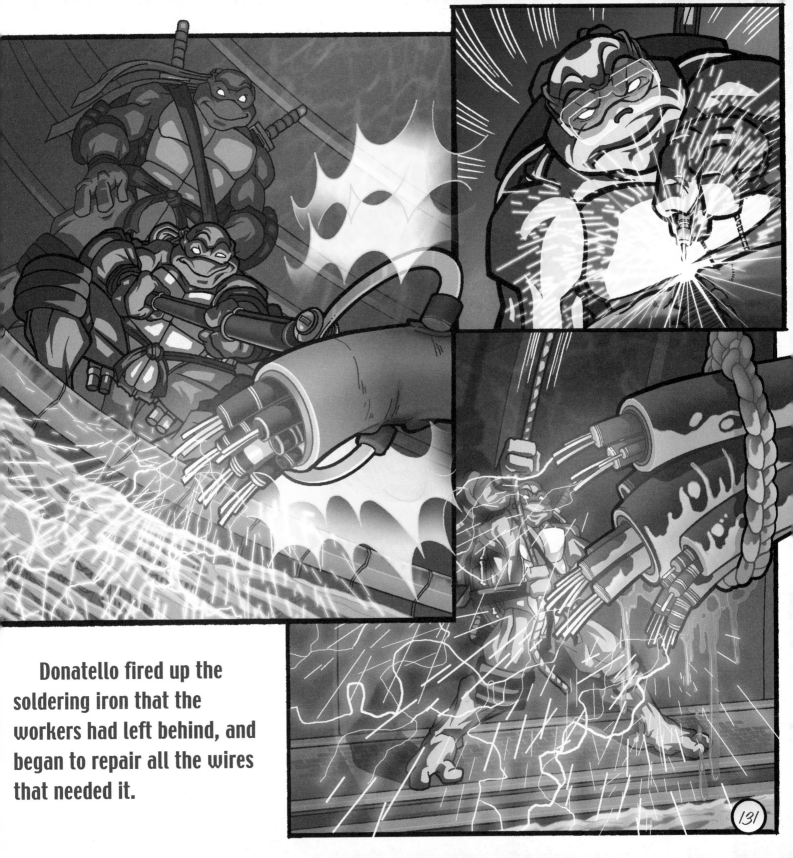

Donatello fired up the soldering iron that the workers had left behind, and began to repair all the wires that needed it.

When Leonardo and Michelangelo returned, Donatello repaired the fallen power line as quickly as he could. "There," he said. "Now I just need to flick the switch in the side panel of the power line box."

"You'd better hurry," said Michelangelo. "It's getting dimmer down here, which means there must be no light coming in from the storm drain above."

Donatello tried to open the panel—but it was stuck!

Michelangelo tried to open the panel but had no luck. Leonardo couldn't open it either.

"What should we do?" asked Leonardo.

"I know!" said Michelangelo, brightening. "I'll give it some Turtle whacks!"

He sprang into the air and delivered the mightiest of kicks to the stubborn panel.

Suddenly the panel burst open!

"Nice work, Mikey," said Donatello, as he reached into the panel and felt around for the switch. When he found it, he flicked it on, and everything brightened a little.

"You saved the day, Mikey!" said Donatello.

"He saved the city, too," Leonardo called from the distance. Michelangelo and Donatello went over to see.

Donatello and Michelangelo found Leonardo peering out of the manhole. They poked their heads out to see for themselves. It was night, and the entire city was lit up—including the hospital!

"Way to go, Donatello!" Michelangelo cheered. "You sure do know your stuff."

"Sorry I was so snappy before," Donatello apologized.

"I deserved it," said Michelangelo. "I cleaned up your workshop to make up for it."

Donatello was impressed at how well Michelangelo had cleaned his workshop.

"I bet you can fix your whatchamacallit in no time," said Michelangelo. "By the way, what is it?"

"It was going to be a device to help us set off a stink bomb in the heating system at Foot Headquarters," said Donatello. "But maybe I can turn it into a VCR clock-setting device."

TEENAGE MUTANT NINJA TURTLES™

Four's a Crowd

One night at the Turtles' lair Master Splinter was leading the Teenage Mutant Ninja Turtles in a teamwork exercise. At least he was *trying* to lead.

"Hey!" shouted Leonardo. "You're supposed to work *with* me, Raphael!"

"But my way is better!" Raphael shouted back.

"Guys! Chill out!" yelled Michelangelo, trying to calm them down.

"Raph, you don't know the first thing about teamwork!" exclaimed Leonardo, angrily.

"Maybe I don't need a team!" replied Raphael.

"Well, maybe we don't need you, either!" Leonardo shouted.

"Good! I quit!" Raphael exclaimed and stormed out. The others tried to stop him, but Master Splinter held them back.

"He must choose his own path," Splinter explained, "wherever it takes him."

Raphael headed to the rooftops. He leaped from building to building with only the moonlight to guide him. He was alone. No one could boss him around anymore.

Who needs those guys anyway?, he thought to himself.

Back at the lair the next problem popped up on the monitors.

"Um, guys, check this out," Donatello said, pointing to the screens. There were Hun and some Foot Ninjas breaking into the museum.

"We have to stop them!" Leonardo exclaimed.
"Without Raphael?" asked Michelangelo.
"You have no choice," answered Splinter.

147

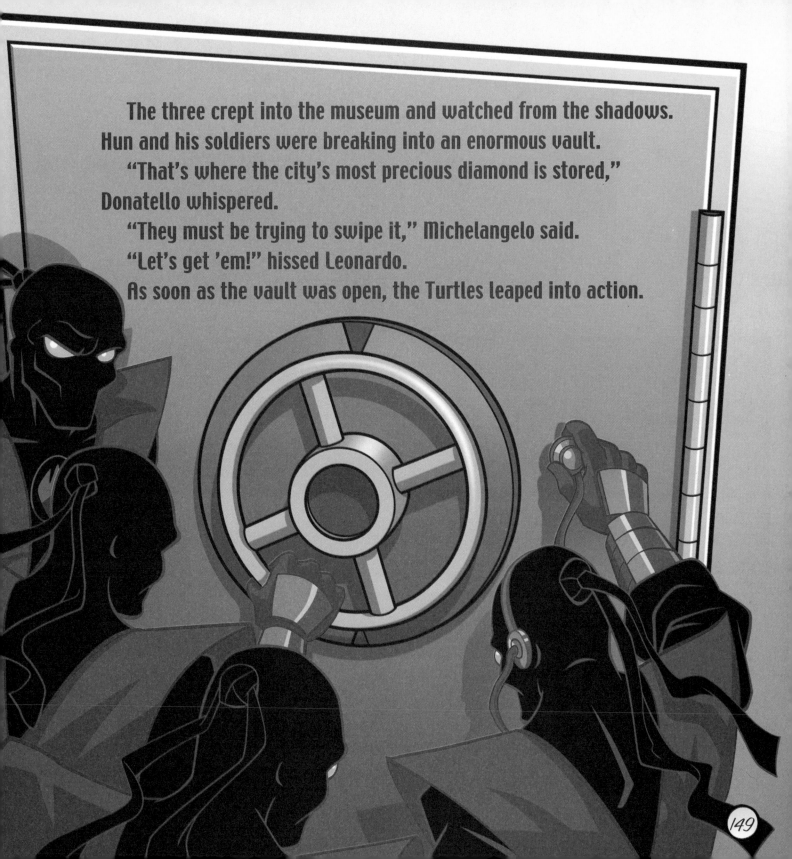

The three crept into the museum and watched from the shadows. Hun and his soldiers were breaking into an enormous vault.

"That's where the city's most precious diamond is stored," Donatello whispered.

"They must be trying to swipe it," Michelangelo said.

"Let's get 'em!" hissed Leonardo.

As soon as the vault was open, the Turtles leaped into action.

Leonardo

SMASHED!

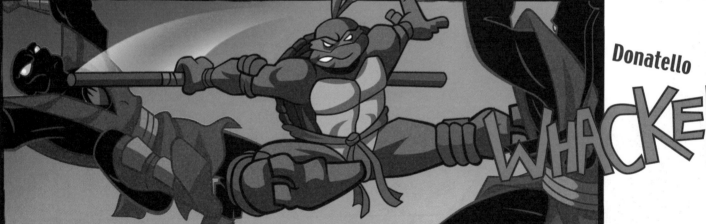

Donatello

WHACKED!

Michelangelo

ROLLED!

But there was no one to get Hun.
"Looks like you are one Turtle too short!" shouted Hun.
He laughed and slammed the vault shut.

The Turtles were trapped.

Master Splinter saw everything on the monitors. He reached for his Shell Cell phone and said, "Raphael, your brothers need you . . . the museum . . . hurry!"

But Splinter was not sure if he heard the message. Raphael did not answer.

The air in the vault was quickly running out.
"I guess this is it," Donatello gasped.
"Save your breath," said Leonardo.
"For what?" asked Michelangelo.

154

"For some serious shelling!" Raphael answered, as he threw open the vault's door. Air rushed into the room. The Turtles got to their feet.

"If it wasn't for you, we'd be goners!" Leonardo cried.

"But we all need to work together to stop Hun," said Raphael.

"Making up is totally sweet," Michelangelo interrupted. "But putting the smackdown on the bad guys would be even sweeter!"

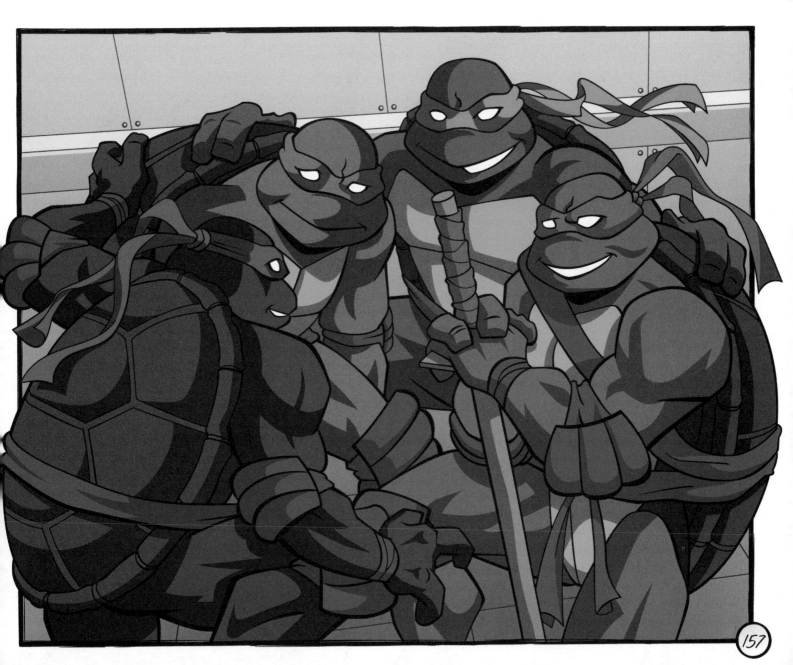

Hun and his gang were busy stealing as many artifacts as they could carry. But outside the museum Donatello, Leonardo, and Michelangelo were waiting for them to try to escape.

"You three aren't enough to stop me!" Hun gloated.

"Good thing there are *four* of us!" cried Raphael, as he swooped down and snatched the diamond.

159

With all four Turtles working together the Foot Ninjas didn't stand a chance.

Hun managed to creep away, but without any of the artifacts he was after . . . or any of his soldiers.

Later that night Splinter welcomed Raphael back to the lair. "The path of success lies with your family," Splinter said softly.

"I know that now," answered Raphael.

"Me too," said Leonardo.

"Awesome!" said Michelangelo. "So who in this family is making me dinner?"

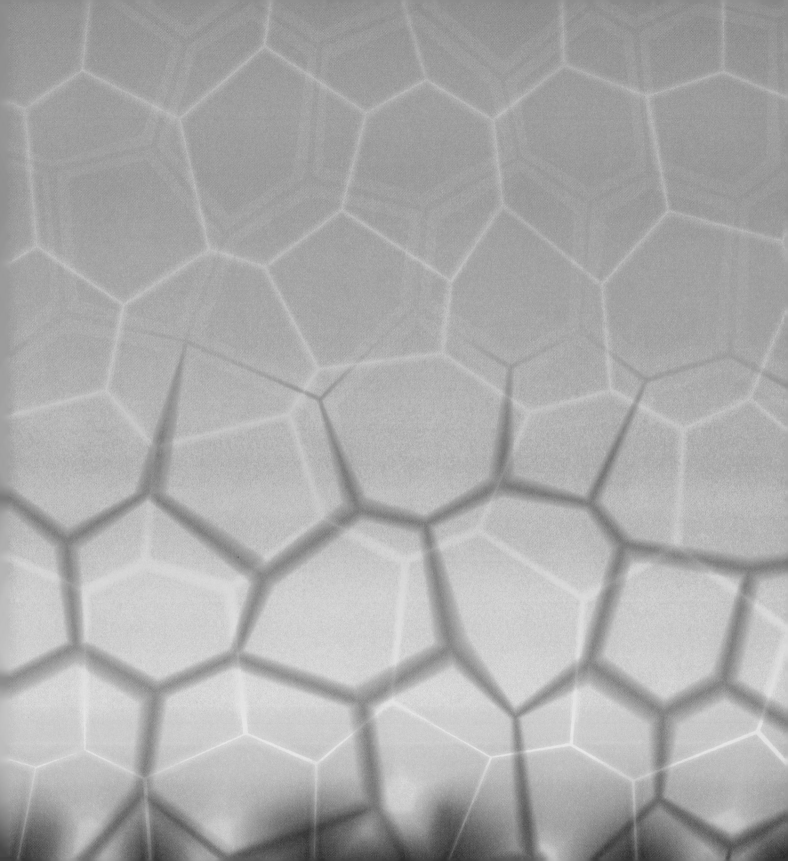

Michelangelo stared into the dark pool that led to the sewers. "I wish I were in my room reading comic books," he said.

"But I need your help, Mikey," said Donatello, holding up a steel pipe. "I need you to secure this pipe into the underwater entryway, so it won't close up when we cruise through in a submersible."

"Got it!" said Michelangelo. He grabbed the pipe and jumped in.

Michelangelo swam down to the entryway and put the steel pipe in place. Then he froze with fear! There in front of him was a large, crocodile-like creature. It had human arms and legs, razor-sharp teeth, and a green, spiked tail. The croc roared!

Get a grip, Michelangelo told himself. Splinter would tell me to relax and fade into the background. As soon as the croc turned away, Michelangelo quickly swam to the surface.

Michelangelo found all three of his brothers waiting for him. "You'll . . . never . . . believe . . . what I saw!" he said breathlessly. "It was part crocodile . . . part human!"

"I think Mikey's lost it!" said Raphael.

"It *really* exists!" insisted Michelangelo. "Come see for yourselves."

When the other Turtles refused to go, Donatello gave Michelangelo a scuba mask with a two-way radio and an underwater propulsion device. "The camera and transmitter will let us see your 'mystery croc' on our plasma screen . . . *if* it exists," he explained.

"Stay tuned, guys," said Michelangelo. "Mikey TV is taking you on a croc hunt!"

While underwater, Michelangelo saw the croc
near the entryway with a mechanical part in its mouth.

"I take it back, Mikey," Raphael said into the radio. "You're not insane."

"The chase is on!" said Michelangelo. He followed the croc to a place that looked *very* familiar. "Guys," he said, "you're never going to believe where I am!"

"Mikey's in our old lair!" said Donatello, staring at the plasma screen. "Big, dark, and scaly is living in our old home."

They watched as the croc stood on two legs and put on a lab coat and glasses.

"It's a big crocodile version of Don!" said Leonardo. "Look at his workshop!"

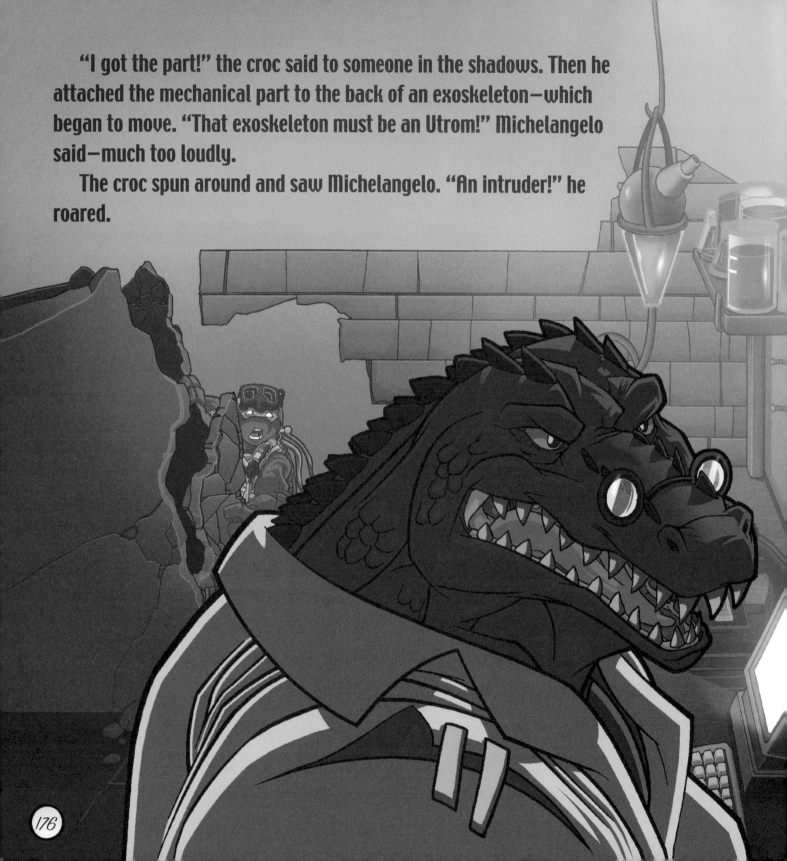

"I got the part!" the croc said to someone in the shadows. Then he attached the mechanical part to the back of an exoskeleton—which began to move. "That exoskeleton must be an Utrom!" Michelangelo said—much too loudly.

The croc spun around and saw Michelangelo. "An intruder!" he roared.

"N-nice crocodile . . . ," said Michelangelo, backing out of the lair. The croc charged at him, and for a while they struggled. Then the croc bit the propulsion device off Michelangelo's back, flung him several feet, and whacked him with its tail.

"Mikey! Mikey!" cried Raphael. But there was no answer.

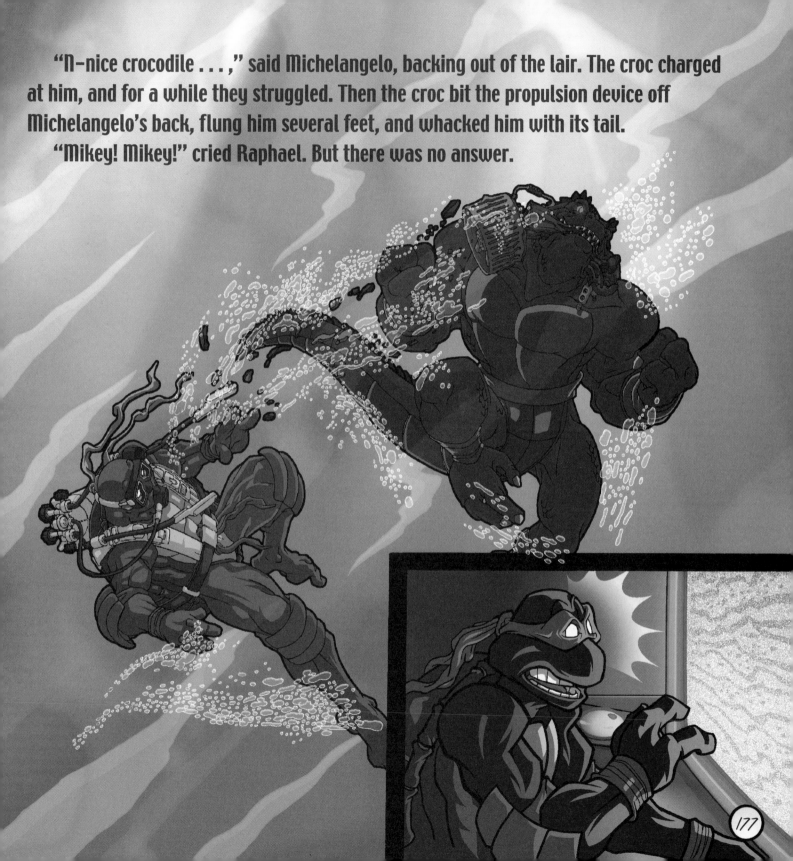

While Michelangelo prepared to use his nunchaku, the croc became more human again. "I . . . I . . . am sorry," he said. "I got carried away."

Just then the Sewer Slider arrived. The Turtles jumped out, ready for action.

"It's okay, guys," said Michelangelo. "Croc and I are calling a truce."

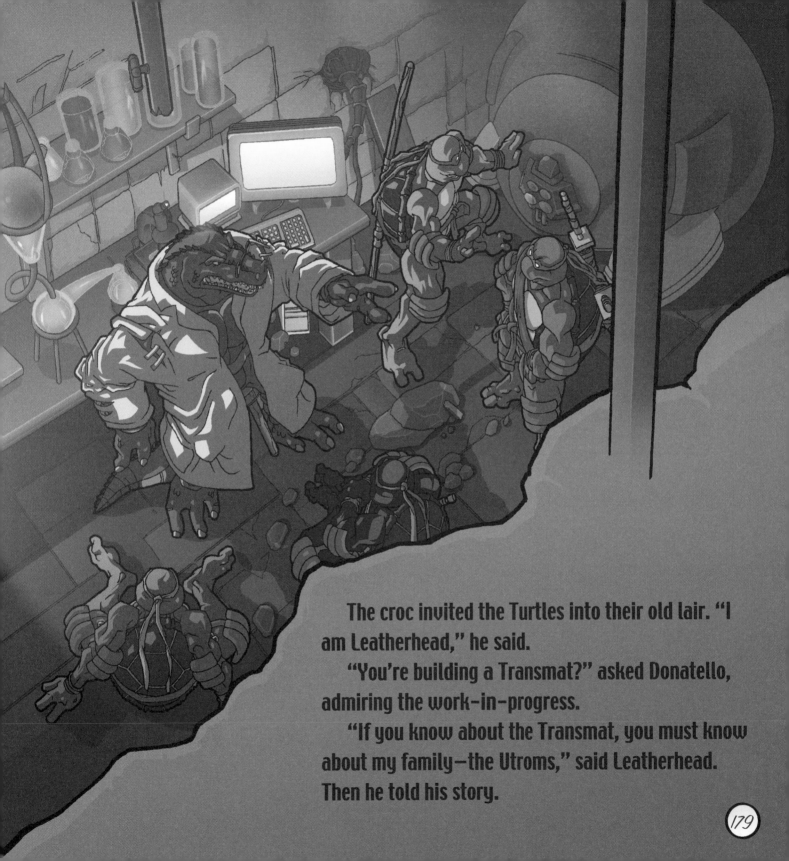

The croc invited the Turtles into their old lair. "I am Leatherhead," he said.

"You're building a Transmat?" asked Donatello, admiring the work-in-progress.

"If you know about the Transmat, you must know about my family—the Utroms," said Leatherhead. Then he told his story.

"I was once a pet that was thrown into the sewer," said Leatherhead. "The Utroms brought me to their home, where I was accidentally exposed to a mutagen. It affected my body and made me highly intelligent. The Utroms barely escaped when humans tried to destroy them. Once I finish building this Transmat, I'll finally be able to join my family again."

Just then an exoskeleton appeared in the doorway. The Turtles couldn't believe their eyes! Inside the exoskeleton's chest cavity was a jar that contained Baxter Stockman's head. "Don't trust those Turtles!" Stockman shouted. "They betrayed the Utroms!"

"He's a liar!" said Michelangelo. Leatherhead didn't know who to believe.

"It's time to put our anti-Turtle device to work!" said Stockman. He tossed some shapes into the air. They split apart, expanded, and joined together to form a Turtlebot!

"This doesn't look good," said Donatello. He spun his bo staff and stepped toward the Turtlebot. But the Turtlebot knocked him off his feet.

Michelangelo swung his nunchaku, but the Turtlebot blocked it again and again.

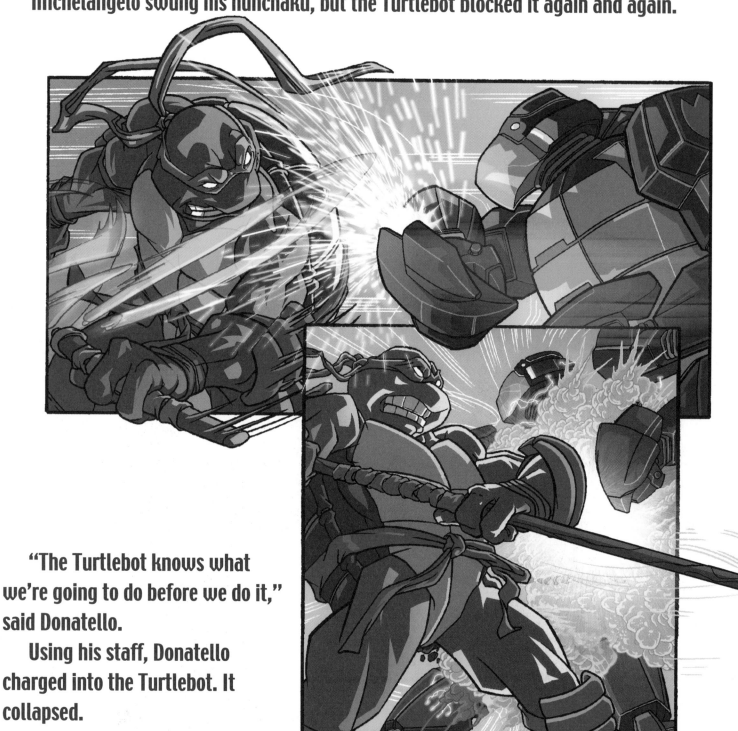

"The Turtlebot knows what we're going to do before we do it," said Donatello.

Using his staff, Donatello charged into the Turtlebot. It collapsed.

Stockman furiously slammed the Turtles—two at a time—to the floor.

"I've wanted my revenge ever since I worked for Shredder," said Stockman.

"You worked for Shredder?" Leatherhead asked, becoming angry. "You were never going to help me with the Transmat. Shredder was the Utroms' worst enemy!"

Stockman hurled a gas cylinder that burst into flames when it hit the ceiling of the lair. *Boom!*

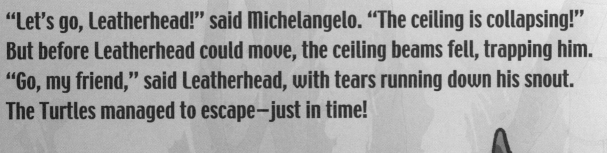

"Let's go, Leatherhead!" said Michelangelo. "The ceiling is collapsing!"
But before Leatherhead could move, the ceiling beams fell, trapping him.
"Go, my friend," said Leatherhead, with tears running down his snout.
The Turtles managed to escape—just in time!

"Poor Leatherhead," Michelangelo said sadly. "He was so alone."
"I wish we could have saved him," added Leonardo.
"Things sure get rough at times," said Donatello. "But at least we have each other."